Little Miss Lorelai Loves the Sea

By Lisa Peters

ISBN-978-0-578-75082-8
Library of Congress Control Number 2020914653

Editing by Stella Joy
Illustrations by Lisa Peters

Printed and bound in the United States of America
First Printing August 2020
Published by Dean Diaries LLC

**To order additional copies
of this book, contact the author**:

Lisa Peters
https://mailchi.mp/c1e1d08f3672/little-miss-lorelai-loves-the-sea

This book is dedicated to and inspired by my amazing children, Kanen and Lorelai. You inspire me with your insatiable curiosity, creative imaginations and love of life. I love you both, with all my heart!

Little Miss Lorelai loves the sea! She frolics, plays and giggles with glee!

She makes some friends great and small.

She explores, collects and inspects them all.

She smiles at a Tuna fish so powerful and strong.

Then, she waves at a starfish so gentle and calm.

She collects a sand dollar, a minnow, a slug, a seahorse, a crab and a clam that dug!

She fills a bucket with water and sand. And, makes them a home so comfy and grand!

She names each one and tries to be fair, in treating them all with respect and care.

Before too long, she hears a faint sound.

Sandy the sand dollar cries out with a frown, "Oh please, oh please, listen to me. We aren't meant for a bucket; we live in the sea!"

Then, Hermie the hermit crab says with a pinch, "I need seaweed and currents and to hide in a trench!"

Suzie the seahorse says with a song, "I'm meant to dance and gallop all day long, in caves of coral and soft anemone, with other friends that are just like me!"

Marky the minnow exclaims with a sigh, "Oh no, oh no, oh my, oh my! There's nowhere for me to swim and play, stuck here in this bucket all day!"

Sid the slug just mopes around, feeling so sad and making no sound.

While Kanen the clam digs deep in the sand, hoping to escape that giant hand!

How might she feel if she were them? Would she feel lost, lonely, or miss her brother, Tim?

She knew the answer right away, in her bucket, they could not stay.

Although she was sad to say good-bye, she knew their place was in the sea with the rest of their friends and family.

"We are pleased to have met you and to make your acquaintance. You've shown us great love and kindness and patience."

With a wave of her hand and a kiss in the wind, she says a fond farewell to each new friend.

She releases them back to the deep blue sea,
where they all swam away, so wild and free…
Just exactly where they're meant to be!

Acknowledgements

My profound appreciation goes to a few people that helped me through this two-year journey. This book would not have come to fruition without them. I am eternally grateful to you all!

First and foremost, my awesome husband, Zach. I love you! Thank you for your unceasing encouragement, love and support. I am so very blessed to have you. You're the best!

Sierra D. and her team at Dean Diaries, for guiding me along the self-publishing process and always ready to answer a million questions.

Also to Rob B., Mariel L. and Laura M. for your invaluable artistic advice and instruction.

Thanks to Cori M. and Jess E. for helping me with the finishing touches.

To my mom for… well, everything, I love you lots!

My nieces and nephews, each of you holds a special place in my heart. I cannot wait to see where life takes you.

"Little Miss Lorelai Loves the Sea"
was written on the beach in Destin, Florida.

To see the video that inspired this book and meet the
real Little Miss Lorelai go to:
https://www.instagram.com/littlemisslorelailovesthesea/

Made in the USA
Monee, IL
04 November 2020